PADDY
THE
FLYING PIG

by
Caius Julyan

Illustrations by
Frances Schofield

For Ron, Eithne, Chitrita, Mia & Niall

Contents

Ireland, as everybody knows, is a little country.
It's faced its fair share of troubles over the centuries and its
people are, consequently, a plain-speaking and tough lot.
They have produced great Presidents…and great poets.
They love a party…but aren't scared of a fight.
But they are also funny…kind…clever…and wise.
If you become a hero in Ireland – you're a hero forever.

This is the story of one such hero…. and it begins not so
very long ago, when many houses had straw roofs, the peat
that was burned for fuel could be smelled everywhere
…and *everyone* went to Mass on a Sunday.

CHAPTER 1
A Summer's Day

In one small village lived an old lady called Mrs McGuirk. From the time she had been a little girl she had always lived on the same farm in Termonfeckin – that's the name of the village – with a few cows, some geese, ducks, one old horse and her pet pig. The farmhouse was of a simple and elegant design common thereabouts, was quite large and sat at the top of a fir tree-lined winding driveway. Either side of it, there were a few acres of pasture which sloped gently away down to a stream which burbled away all year long.

Termonfeckin was – and is – the kind of village which was just small enough for everyone to know everyone else – and at the same time just large enough to avoid the neighbours, nice though they were, if you felt like it. In other words, it was just like a hundred other villages the length and breadth of Ireland!

On the day our story begins, the weather was grand. It was hot; bees buzzed slowly from flower to flower and Jenny, the old mare, was standing as still as she could at the gate, occasionally flicking her ears or swishing her tail to shoo away the flies. And as Mrs McGuirk lazed in her favourite garden chair (which was in fact an old moth-eaten armchair she'd thrown out years ago), she listened to the cows slowly scrunching and munching on endless mouthfuls of delicious Irish grass.

And somewhere nearby, Mrs McGuirk could just make out the sounds of her 9-year-old Grand-nephew, Aidan, thrashing away at something or other with a stick and half-singing a song he vaguely knew – and she vaguely half-recognised.

And she thought to herself that at that very moment, she had never been as happy and contented. Well, *almost*. The *only* thing, she realized, that could make the day *perfect* in every way was if that annoying, snorty snoring coming from somewhere nearby would stop – even for just a *few* minutes!

She shaded her eyes from the sun and squinted in the direction of the noise and there, under the big hedge that separated the garden from the fields beyond, lay Paddy – one of the biggest, idlest and silliest pigs you ever saw.

"Paddy!", Mrs McGuirk snapped. "Will you please stop that awful racket and give me some peace?!"

Paddy woke up with a start, snorting loudly and struggled, befuddled, to his feet. He stood there for a moment, dazed and half asleep and wondering – not for the first time – what it was he'd done wrong now.

"Why don't you make yourself useful and go for a walk – or something? Surely there's no other pig in the whole of Ireland that sleeps as much as you do. Now go on, off you go!"

And Paddy, idle and slow-witted though he was, understood perfectly well when he was not wanted and decided it would be best for all concerned if he did indeed take himself off for a walk.

Paddy had been cared for by Mrs McGuirk since he was tiny. In return, he loved Mrs McGuirk more than he would ever be able to tell her. After all, there were few other people in Termonfeckin – or indeed anywhere – who would have fed, watered and yes, *loved* him all these years and expected so little in return. And he hoped that Mrs McGuirk could see from the look in his eyes, and the way he slightly drooped his head that he was sorry that he'd upset her.

And – maybe – a walk wasn't such bad idea after all? Now that he came to think of it, he couldn't really remember the last time he'd stirred himself to go any-where. And on a day like this, he thought, he knew just the place to go: the stream at the bottom of Mrs McGuirk's field.

Seeing Paddy amble off, Aidan piped up:

"Granny - I'm off for a walk as well – I'll keep an eye on Paddy for you!"

"Grand, Aidan – stay out of mischief and be back here for supper. I don't want to have to come looking for you!"

But Aidan heard none of this, as he was already off through the garden gate and following Paddy at a discreet distance. Aidan came to stay with Mrs McGuirk most summers. She and his actual Grandmother were sisters, who he lived with across country in Tipperary which, as everyone knows, is a long way from just about everywhere. Aidan's parents were both long dead and his grandmother had raised him alone since he was tiny.

Aidan loved both his Grannies – but he *especially* loved his summer holidays here in Termonfeckin…even if there wasn't always much to do….

But today, there was: Aidan suddenly felt quite grown-up as Paddy's self-appointed bodyguard.

10 minutes or so after setting off, Paddy found himself standing under the shade of some trees next to a babbling stream, wheezing and very hot. Happily, there was a little mud here and there at the edge of the water for him to roll around in and generally cool down a degree or two.

Aidan, meanwhile, not wishing to frighten or disturb dear old Paddy, had found a thicket of tall grass nearby and had lain down in it to wait…

But it was at almost exactly this moment – as thoughts slowly bumped up against each other in Paddy's mind, his mouth ajar – 'gawping', Mrs McGuirk called it – that he realized he was staring at a trail of tiny footprints dotted in the mud all around him. And just as he was on the verge of transforming this information into an actual thought – his attention was caught by what sounded like a very distant shout.

"*Help*!!"

Paddy looked around him and twitched his ears. Aidan playing in a neighbouring field, or down in the village perhaps?

"*Heeeeeellp*!!!!"

Paddy's head jerked in the opposite direction – the voice wasn't coming from far away at all, but from somewhere closer – much closer.

"For the love of God, over here you *eejit*!!!"

Paddy's head twitched back again, almost to the position it had originally been in while gawping.

"That's it ! Over here…yes, *here*!"

Everything at that moment happened so quickly, Paddy thought later, that he didn't even have time to get scared. Paddy's eyes finally focussed on the source of the shouty little voice; not Aidan at all - but a tiny red-faced little man clinging to a rock for all he was worth in the middle of the fast-flowing stream. If he wasn't rescued very quickly *indeed*, he'd almost certainly be swept away and drowned.

"Don't just stand there – get me out of here", he screeched, "*NOW*!!!"

Before Paddy knew what he was doing, he was knee-deep in water and face to face with the little fellow. As if by instinct, he pressed his nose to the rock, where a pair of the smallest green legs you've ever seen were doing a jig in mid-air. The next thing Paddy was aware of was that he was wading ashore with a little man clinging to the end of his nose.

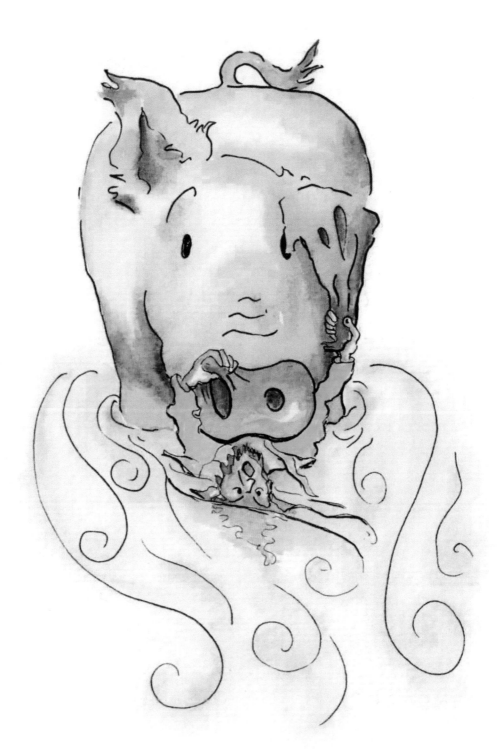

"*Owwwww*!!! Be careful, you great lump: I've done myself a mischief
and I don't need *you* making it worse than it already is. Now put me down over
there – and don't drop me, or you'll know all about it!"

Well, it was only when Paddy had finally deposited his tiny new passenger on
the bank of the stream that he began to realize just what it was that he had done.
He looked down and took a very long, hard look at the smallest person he had
ever seen.

And the only explanation he had - was that *this*…. was a *fairy*.

CHAPTER 2
One Magic Wish... Or Two?

Aidan had been on the point of drifting off to sleep, enveloped as he was by the gently swaying grass and the heavy, warm air…when he thought he heard what sounded like a voice…a very small cross voice…

But who's? Paddy had wandered alone into the thicket of small trees and undergrowth next to the stream…. but there *was* no one else around.
Staying as still as he could, Aidan waited….and listened.

* * *

Sure, Paddy had heard Mrs McGuirk and plenty of other people laughing and joking about fairies plenty of times before – but had any of them ever seen one in the flesh? It was nothing short of incredible…

"Well, *you* took your time!", said the little fellow, as he sat on the bank, squeezing the water out of his hat. Paddy's jaw drooped a little further from its usual *gawping* position. "Another minute in there and I would have been drowned-ed, so I would. And then what would the *rest* of the little people have done without their King?" Paddy was just about to attempt, for the second time in just a matter of minutes,

to turn everything he was hearing into something he could understand –
when he was again distracted from this task by the little man barking at him.

"Right! That's quite enough idling about – I don't have time for it *and* I can't
bear people – or pigs – that do it. My leg hurts something *dreadful* and I want
to go home. Now are you going to stand there like a half-wit – or help me?"

Paddy's jaw snapped shut – which, to the Fairy King at least, seemed to suggest
that Paddy was willing to do as he was commanded.

The small wood that surrounds the stream at the bottom of Mrs McGuirk's field
had never been properly explored by Paddy. This was partly because, as a pig,
it wasn't something he tended to do a lot of – and secondly, because all the land –
including the farmhouse and the stream – belonged to Colm Quigley.
And Colm, was not a man on who's land one poked one's nose – piggy *or* human
– where it was most certainly not wanted.

But that's quite enough about Colm Quigley – for now.

With the Fairy King once again holding tight onto Paddy's hooter and shouting
directions – mixed with a few choice insults – Paddy had somehow stumbled through
the water, weeds and undergrowth and now found himself in a small clearing….

"Stop here!" Shouted the little man. "Don't move a *muscle*".

And scrambling upright, still perched atop Paddy's snout, the King held up his
hand – as though commanding the entire wood to hold its breath. And then blew a
whistle so loud, it was hard to believe someone so small could make such a *racket*!

"Phweeeeeeeeeet!!!" he went. And again, "*Phweeeeeeeeeeeeeeeeeeeeeeettt*!!!!"

In the blink of an eye Paddy suddenly realized that everything around him was
alive. Every branch, every toadstool and every moss-covered rock and stone was
teeming with movement. Paddy couldn't count, but he knew what a lot was – and
here were a *lot* of little people all scrambling down from, and out of, their places
of concealment, hurrying to surround their Fairy King and this mud-spattered
four-legged stranger with him.

"Ahem!" said the King, clearing his throat and puffing himself up to his full
height – a little *too* grandly, Paddy thought to himself.

"My dear fairies. I stand here before you as a King who is lucky to be here at all. Only a short while ago, I faced my *blackest* hour!"

At these words, there was an audible gasp from the assembled, spellbound throng. Sensing the impression he was making, the King continued in a similarly theatrical vein:

"But at the very moment I feared all was lost – a knight in shining armour appeared before me and delivered me from certain death!"

Two hundred pairs of tiny eyes swivelled as one towards Paddy. His jaw snapped shut as he realized he was now the centre of attention.

"This pig is nothing less than a *hero*, so he is", said the King - and he went on to tell the fairies about his terrible accident and extraordinary rescue that had just occurred – emphasising, of course, his own fortitude & forbearance whilst facing certain doom. Finally, he said:

"Now, I have decided, as your King, that we must show our gratitude by bestowing on this noble swine such gifts as you, my subjects, deem a worthy reward for such bravery!"

As these last, fine words rang out from the King, the crowd erupted into *pandemonium*! They cheered and clapped, threw tiny hats into the air and generally let it be known that Paddy's rescue of their King was indeed a tremendous and wonderful event, deserving of the *highest* praise. And as for Paddy – well, he was elated and as happy as he could ever remember being. He had never been praised for anything in his life before unless you counted thanks for *stopping* doing something – like snoring. And they were *even* going to give him some 'gifts', whatever they were.

The cheering was brought to an abrupt end by the King, as he waved his arms and forced himself to be heard above the racket.

"Right then", he said "any suggestions?"
"A year's supply of carrots!", shouted one fairy.
"A waistcoat!", yelled another.
"Wellingtons…cabbage leaves…tennis racket…a roof rack!",
were all suggestions.

But none of these seemed right *at all* to the King – even though the cabbage leaves sounded just fine to Paddy. But the frown on the King's face seemed to suggest a frustration – irritation, even – with his subjects. After all, he had been close to perishing – and his rescuer should be honoured accordingly.

"I have it!", he suddenly burst out.
"There is only one wish that will do – a magic wish!"

For the second time in as many minutes, Paddy heard a gasp of wonder ripple through the crowd. The King then turned to Paddy with a flourish:

"Well young fella – what's it to be, then? What is your heart's desire? What in the whole *wide* world would you most like to have – or do?"

Poor Paddy. Never in all his long, carefree days in Mrs McGuirk's back garden had he ever been confronted with a decision bigger than whether it was time to eat…. or sleep. He realized that he ought to try and explain this to the King and all the fairies when a terrible thought struck him: he would *never* be able to explain anything to *anyone* – because he couldn't *speak*!

But Kings are Kings for a reason, and seeing Paddy's obvious confusion, he snapped his fingers and shouted:

"Pig, I hereby grant you the Power of Speech – for today and all the days that stretch ahead of you!"

"What do you mean?", said Paddy.

"I mean", said the King "…that henceforth you are blessed with the ability to communicate through language. See?"

"No, I don't see at all, I'm not………". Paddy's voice trailed off.

He was speaking. He was talking…

"I'm talking! I'm a *talking* pig, so I am!"

CHAPTER 3

If Pigs Could Fly

Well, you've never heard such noise. Gales of laughter swept through, around and out of the crowd of fairies. Even the King was bent double, tears rolling down his ruddy cheeks. Some of the fairies looked as if they would faint with exhaustion they laughed so much. And Paddy too was soon gasping for air as he spluttered and choked with sheer happiness. Eventually, the King was able to regain his composure and waved his arms for quiet....

"Enough, *enough*!", he shouted. And when order was finally restored, he continued:

"In fairness, my friends, the pig didn't choose to be able to speak, so technically he may – if he so wishes – still exercise his right to make a magic wish. But before we ask him to choose, I have a very important question for him; pig – what's your name?"

"Well, er I...I don't know really. I've never called myself anything, really...". Paddy had never spoken before and his first attempt, a barely audible rasping whisper, made him sound like he had just given up smoking.

His voice trailed off in embarrassment.

"Oh, come now, my fine fellow – everyone has a name – apart from me of course; I'm just 'Your Majesty' most of the time. What do your *friends* call you?"
"I don't have any friends...well, I have Mrs McGuirk....and young Aidan, I suppose...Mrs McGuirk's not really my *friend* – but she *does* look after me. She calls me.... Paddy".

There was a pause, while the King (and all the fairies) digested this information. And then:

"Grand!", said the King. "That's a *fine* name for a pig – and especially one as bold and brave as you – *Paddy*".

Once again, applause rippled around the crowd of fairies, as if to signify their approval of this fine Irish name being associated with this *finest* of Irish pigs.

"Paddy, it is now time for you to make your real wish", said the King.
"What, in the whole wide world would you *most* like to have – or do?"

Paddy felt very unsure of what to say next. He wanted to make a wish, of course, but didn't want to disappoint the fairies by choosing something boring…or silly. After all, everyone had been so kind to him.

Feeling increasingly anxious, he turned to the King and said
"What do *you* think I should choose?"
"Paddy, it's not for me to choose *for* you – isn't there *anything* you've *always* wished you'd been able to do; ride a bike, speak French, tell jokes – wear a blazer – there must be *something*??!!"

Paddy shuffled from foot to foot and stared down at the ground.
The King was right; there must be something, but *what*? Pigs don't generally spend a lot of time wishing for things…

"Well, there is *one* thing, I suppose…", he mumbled hoarsely, hardly daring to look the King in the eye.

"I…I've always wondered what it must be like to….to *fly*".

There's was a second's silence, followed by the King virtually shouting
"That's it, flying! What a wonderful suggestion Paddy – it's genius, a *flying pig* – whoever would've thought of that?!?"

And in the blink of an eye, while Paddy was still collecting his thoughts and half-wondering whether there wasn't something better he could have chosen – like having perfect mud to wallow in all year-round or an endless supply of turnips – the King had waved his arms over Paddy's head, muttered a few mysterious words and told him that the magic would take a few, short minutes to take effect….but that until it did, Paddy was to be the Guest of Honour at a great party!

Straight away, the King decreed that The Great Hall was the only venue suitable for an event of this importance. And before he knew what was happening, Paddy found himself being pushed & pulled forward by hundreds of tiny hands until he found himself in front of one of the tiniest doors he had ever seen – no bigger than the cat flap in Mrs McGuirk's kitchen door.

"Paddy", said the King, "as our most-honoured guest, I bid you enter!"

Well, you probably don't need me to tell you what happened next.

The lovely little door, so beautifully hidden amongst the tangled roots of a great oak tree was just that little bit too…well, *little*. Paddy pushed…and twisted…and heaved…turned and squirmed – but there was nothing that he, the King or scores of fairies could do to get him through it.

Finally, just as it appeared that there was going to be no party after all, the King said: "I have an idea – if Paddy can't come to the party - then the party must come to *Paddy*!"

Suddenly, music and dancing erupted all around Paddy. Weaving around his legs, dancing, singing and shouting were scores of his new little friends having the time of their lives. Drinks were served in acorn cups; tables made from twigs were suddenly heaving with all kinds of strange foods and Paddy was amazed to see these tiny people buzz through the air and even change colour to blend in with the plants and trees around them.

It was wonderful. It was so wonderful, in fact, that Paddy had completely forgotten about his new magical powers – and it was in the middle of him joining in with a rousing chorus of '*Michael Finnegan*', that Paddy became aware of a fairy he hadn't noticed before fluttering and hovering in front of his face.

"Well Paddy – do you know how to fly yet?"
"Er, no…I mean, I want to, but I don't know how….
maybe you could show me, er…"
"Orla", said Orla. "I suppose *I* could help you…. I'm *probably* the best flyer around here. Shall we start, pig?"
"I suppose so", said Paddy, who still wasn't *completely* sure whether he *really* wanted to fly…especially as 'Orla' seemed rather bossy.

So, while the party continued noisily around them, Orla began:

"First, you must close your eyes…. then twirl your tail and flap your ears – all at the same time".

This sounded almost impossible to Paddy. But he thought he'd better show willing. He closed his eyes, started twirling his tail and tried flapping his ears as best he could. He peeped out of one eye. Nothing.

"Keep trying, Paddy – you'll soon get the hang of it, I promise…".

And with all his might, Paddy flapped and twirled for all he was worth, until after what seemed like an age he said:

"This is exhaustipating, Orla – I'm getting awful tired….".

And it was then that he heard a little faraway voice say:

"I think you'd better open your eyes now Paddy".

Ever so gently Paddy opened his eyes. Down below him he could just see Orla, the wood, the stream where he'd rescued the King and hundreds of by-now cheering little people! He was so surprised that for a split-second he forgot to keep twirling his tail and started falling towards the crowd below him.

"Keep twirling Paddy – concentrate!!!" shouted Orla and a dozen other voices up at him. "You're doing great!!!"

And Paddy *was* doing great. In just a few minutes he began to get the hang of flapping his ears and twirling his tail at the same time – even how to flap one ear a little more than the other, allowing him to change direction. By now the fairies were applauding each new twist and turn Paddy mastered…and a few of the drunker ones were even shouting up the odd suggestion of what he might try next:

"Loop the loop, fella!" "Show us a dive bomb!", and whatnot. Paddy couldn't *believe* it. In a day packed with incredible events, this had to be the most incredible. He was a hero…he had made new friends…and now that he was getting the hang of swooping and soaring, rolling, and diving, he was *indeed* Paddy the Flying Pig.

But all good things must come to an end. It was eventually time for Paddy to wend his way home; after all, Mrs McGuirk would probably be starting to get his dinner ready.

"Paddy", said the King, who had wandered over to say goodbye.
"There's something I must say to you before you leave – and it's very important: we Fairies never interfere in the world of humans. If they knew that we really existed – not just in story books – we would be in *great* danger.
You now possess two great gifts. You must use them wisely and only to do good. You can never reveal how you came to have them – is that understood?"

"But what about Mrs McGuirk? And how will I know when it's the right time to fly or speak – or both?"

"Paddy, since I was a little harsh with you when you rescued me, I'll make an exception: you may tell this Mrs McGuirk of yours, but no-one – and I mean *no-one* else. And don't worry about knowing when the time is right – I believe in you Paddy. You'll know when the time is right.
Now enough gassing – off home with you!"

* * *

After straining to hear more of what he thought sounded just like a little voice some time ago, Aidan had heard nothing else of note and had decided to take a leaf out of Paddy's book - and lay back down again. And as he drifted off into a light sleep, his little head was filled with the sounds of laughing, cheering and happy voices all around him. As the afternoon sun slowly began its stately arc west, Aidan opened his eyes, stretched, and began to remember a strange dream he'd been having; a thought quickly displaced by his rumbling tummy – and a sudden excitement about what Granny might feed him for supper…

CHAPTER 4
Mrs McGuirk... and Aidan

No more than 10 minutes-walk away from Aidan's grassy hiding place, Mrs McGuirk lazily stretched her legs and arms as *she* slowly woke up from one of the loveliest afternoon snoozes she could remember. The air was still warm, and she was just about to slip back into a wonderful dream she'd been enjoying about freshly-baked soda bread covered in fresh butter…when she became aware of a strange noise above her head – sort of like a cat purring loudly. And shielding her eyes from the sun, she squinted upwards.

By the time Paddy landed in front of her a moment later, Mrs McGuirk was still shielding her eyes, but her mouth was drooping wide open…

"You know, Mrs McGuirk, that it's rude to *gawp* at people. Isn't that what *you* say all the time? What's the matter – have you never seen a flying pig before?

"I….no…I….", stuttered Mrs McGuirk.
"Well, that's alright then", said Paddy. "Only, by the look of you I'd say you could do with a lovely cup of *tea*. Will I go and put the kettle on for us?"
"I…no…Paddy…. yes".

A couple of hours later over their fourth or fifth cup, Paddy – who'd now got the hang of speaking without sounding horribly unwell - was still busy recounting the day's fantastical events in every tiny detail to an incredulous and delighted Mrs McGuirk; rescuing the fairy King, the singing and dancing, making a wish, learning to talk…and fly. Well, who wouldn't be amazed by such tales…and *tails*, of course.

Aidan, meanwhile, had meandered home, let himself quietly in the back door and had stayed motionless in the hallway, listening to a conversation…. between Granny - and Paddy! So it was *true*; something really *had* happened down at the stream – and now Paddy could speak!?!

And as he listened, his own mouth hanging open, he could just make out some of what Paddy was saying…. something to do with being very brave…and magic wishes….and dancing! Aidan was a bright boy – but at this very moment, he scarcely knew what to think: was he scared? Was he excited?
Maybe – just maybe - he'd know what to think by tomorrow…

* * *

By the time bedtime came around, Mrs McGuirk realized that she could no longer send Paddy off to his muddy sty at the end of the garden, as it was no longer fit for a pig that could talk – and fly. No, from now on Paddy would lead a different life, here with her and Aidan - together and happy under one roof. So, for the first time in his life, Paddy settled down in front of the kitchen fire, as Mrs McGuirk gently closed the door and padded as quietly as she could up to her bedroom.

In the excitement of the last few hours, Mrs McGuirk hadn't given a *thought* to what had become of Aidan. Now, panicked, she gently pushed his bedroom door ajar and there – to her enormous relief – lay a little, shiny-faced boy, snoring gently in his bed.

And downstairs in front of a gently crackling fire, Paddy slowly let his contented eyes close and allowed his head to fill with dreams of all the wonderful things he had seen and done in just one day….and wonder about all the things he was yet to do in the hours, days, weeks, months, and *years* that stretched ahead of him and Mrs McGuirk.

CHAPTER 5
Paddy's New Life
In Termonfeckin

The next few weeks of Paddy & Ida McGuirk's life passed like a dream: the weather was grand, the grass grew long, the few cattle in the field got fatter and something *new* developed – Paddy and Mrs McGuirk grew *even* fonder of each other. Now, instead of nagging her idle pig or banging pots and pans to let him know food was ready – she had *conversations* with him. She even asked his opinion on all sorts of things: 'Should I cut the hay soon? What colour should I paint the front door? Should I become a vegetarian…and what gossip have you heard lately?'. All kinds of questions – all the time. In fact, to be truthful, every now and then, Paddy started to long for his previous life - sleeping, eating, and not thinking very much about anything…

But there was one thing that Paddy & Mrs McGuirk *had* agreed on: that Paddy's solemn promise to tell no-one else about his magical powers was carved in stone. It was a secret they must both take to their graves.

"After all, Paddy", said Mrs McGuirk one day, "if any one of those old biddies down the road found out that I have a flying & talking pig living here – they'd put *you* in a circus and *me* in St Joseph's Rest Home!"

Paddy didn't exactly know who – or what – the 'old biddies' were or what a 'rest home' was, but he was happy to follow Mrs McGuirk's advice.

Paddy felt sorry that he couldn't share his secret with Aidan, but a promise is a promise – and pigs, like us, take them very seriously indeed. Of course, neither Paddy or Mrs McGuirk knew the truth: that Aidan did indeed know something… if not everything. But Aidan was smarter than the average 9-year-old and had come to a decision of his own: he would be returning home soon…and would take his secret with him.

Time passed and some village tongues had started to wag – but not for any reason you might think: Mrs McGuirk now insisted on taking Aidan *and* Paddy with her when she went shopping. More than a few eyebrows were raised the first time she was followed into *McCardle's International Groceries* by an unusually clean pig. Mac, the owner, was agog:

"I…I'm not sure I'm happy with you bringing a pig in here, Ida…ha ha… he could do all sorts of damage…and er, things".

"Don't talk nonsense, Mac McCardle! Paddy is the best-behaved individual in the whole of Termonfeckin. He's helping me decide what we're going to have for supper this evening. Of course, if you'd rather we went shopping down at *Meegan's Fancy Stores*, I'd be happy to oblige!?"

"Oh, ha hahaha – not at all, Ida not *at all* – you and, er, 'Paddy' are always welcome here!"

"Well, I'm glad we've cleared that up. Now, Aidan & Paddy love baked beans – do you have any?"

From then on, Paddy would occasionally go shopping by himself at *McCardle's* – carrying a list and empty bag in his mouth, that the by-now obliging Mac would fill with all the requested items and send Paddy home with the bag of produce clamped between his jaws. For reasons that Mac couldn't quite fathom, he'd taken a liking to his unusual customer – and found himself on more than one occasion pouring out his troubles to Paddy as he scoured the shelves for the various items on Mrs McGuirk's list:

"…. I suppose, if I'm honest with meself Paddy, she was never the woman for me, but I was much younger that I am now and didn't realize that my future lay with fresh meat & vegetables and a comprehensive selection of essential household items…".

After turning his back on love, Mac had settled into his life as a 'confirmed bachelor' – and what time he did spend away from stacking bottles of bleach and sorting through Noggin's the potato seller's latest delivery – he spent indulging his latest passion: a CB radio he'd brought back from a trip to America and fitted in his Morris Minor. He imagined himself driving a vast 50-ton truck across Montana's never-ending highways, hailing other truckers on his radio and warning them about "Bears in the air" or encouraging them with a "10-4 rubber ducky!" Most of these communications fell on deaf ears in the lanes around Termonfeckin, as there was only Laurence Brannigan's delivery van once a week and the odd tractor. And had they even been able to *hear* Mac, none of them would have had the slightest idea what he was talking about. But Mac was happy…and now sharing his inner life with a pig that occasionally came into his shop had brought him a contentment he hadn't known in years…

And Mac wasn't alone; over the weeks, Paddy was seen more and more often around Termonfeckin – sometimes walking alongside Mrs McGuirk & Aidan as she went about her business: shopping, of course, visiting old Father Heaney who'd been unwell lately or the occasional trip on the bus into Drogheda to go to the Post Office. Paddy *never* spoke – and certainly never *flew* – during these outings, maintaining an unusually disciplined and almost military bearing. But by and by, people started to sense that Paddy understood what was being *said* – sometimes by just a tilt of his head, or the way he moved his ears. He was soon part of the daily life of the village and people would greet him as though things had always been that way:

"You're looking well today, Paddy!"
"Morning Paddy – grand weather we're having".
"We're having some people over after Mass on Sunday – be delighted if you, Ida and Aidan could join us?"
"I didn't see you at all last week Paddy – good to see you again". And so on.
Of course, Paddy was delighted with these greetings and on more than one occasion Aidan feared Paddy was about to answer - and cut in quickly on his behalf before he forgot himself – and answered back!

But for now, it was a very happy state of affairs and Mrs McGuirk, for one, sensed that since Paddy's introduction to village life, her neighbours seemed kinder…politer…and happier.

But not *everyone* in Termonfeckin was happy that a *pig* was now a local 'celebrity'.

CHAPTER 6
Two Rogues

Colm Quigley was the sole proprietor of *Quigley's Bar* – the only pub in the village, in which Colm had been overcharging for flat beer, watered-down whiskey and stale snacks for the last 30 years.

The place hadn't seen a paintbrush in 20 and unless something dramatic changed, wouldn't for *another* 20. Colm's customers comprised of local farmers, the potato seller, Noggin – a couple of regular drunks and Father Heaney, who everyone pretended they hadn't seen in there. Colm had been surly, bitter and mean for as long as anyone in Termonfeckin could remember. He'd bought up land and dozens of the smaller houses in the neighbourhood over the years and could be seen knocking angrily on people's doors now and then chasing after rent they could scarcely afford. He didn't care for his customers…and still less for life in the village. And now, with even a *pig* being of more interest to people than spending money in his spit 'n sawdust bar – Colm's blood felt like it was ready to boil over.

But one quiet lunchtime, a different face appeared in *Quigley's Bar* – a man suited, booted and ruddy-faced with a business-like air about him - plonked himself down on one of the less-rickety bar stools and ordered himself a Guinness. Colm eyed him up as he let Ireland's famous stout settle in the pint glass, and he felt he saw a kindred spirit sitting in front of him.

"And what brings you to our humble establishment?", Colm tried for starters.
"Land", said the stranger, as he took a good long draw of his pint."Buying or selling?", ventured Colm, though he guessed the stranger could only be buying – as he knew most of the landowners hereabouts, including, of course, himself.
"Who's asking?"
"Colm Quigley. The proud owner of *Quigley's Bar* – and much else hereabouts! And you are…...?"
"O'Meaney. Tom O'Meaney. Developer and entrepreneur.
Your pub's a dive – but this pint's not bad. Same again!"

Colm bristled inwardly at the insult, but since there were no other customers to enjoy his red-faced discomfort, he decided to press on…

"…and what kind of land would you be looking for, exactly? Perhaps I could help?"
"Maybe…. industrial land. Four, maybe five acres. Enough for a factory, as it happens."
"A factory? We don't have any of those around here. What kind of factory?"
"A sausage factory. There's a ready supply of pigs around here – but *nowhere* to turn them into the finest sausages, chops and bacon in all Ireland!"

Colm suddenly felt as though he was floating 6 feet off the ground while a choir of angels filled the air with the most beautiful music it was possible to imagine. He wasn't a Catholic. He didn't even believe in God. But surely *this* was fate…. it was Heaven rewarding him for his years of lonely & thankless graft!

"The next pint's on me, Mr O'Meaney. *Of all the pubs in all of Ireland, you've been fortunate enough to walk into mine* – ha ha…I think I *might* be able to solve your problem." Tom O'Meaney didn't quite catch Colm's clumsy attempt at warmth, but he paused mid-swig:

"Well? How so?" Over the next 20 minutes, Colm Quigley explained in detail to his new friend that he just so happened to own a 5-acre plot here in Termonfeckin which had *everything* he could possibly need, including a lovely stream at the bottom of the fields into which, he guessed, industrial waste could be pumped.

"Of course, there *is* someone living there now – a weak-minded old woman who keeps a pig as a pet – but I can be rid of her in a heartbeat. Just say the word!"
"You mean, she's just a tenant on your land?", asked O'Meaney, now clearly interested in Colm's proposal.
"I'll *make her an offer she can't refuse* – ah..ha ha ha…", replied Colm, another weak gag failing to make any impression on his prized customer.
"Well, this sounds grand Quigley – but I'm a man in a hurry. I've got another option 10 miles from here and I can do a deal over there in a week's time.
If you can get me what I want faster, I'll cut you in for half a million.
How soon can you get rid of the old woman?"

And Colm, scarcely able to comprehend the sums on offer and desperate to seal the deal of a lifetime, blurted out the first thing that came into his befuddled noggin:

"48 hours. Meet me here Friday at midday and I'll have everything ready!"

And with that, a firm handshake over a bar now littered with empty Guinness glasses, Tom O'Meaney turned on his heels and marched out of the pub, having changed Colm Quigley's life in just one, short hour.

CHAPTER 7
Colm's Generous offer

In the minutes that followed Tom O'Meaney's departure, Colm Quigley was
in a daze: at almost the *exact* moment that he felt he'd had enough of his pub,
Termonfeckin, its dopey inhabitants and their fawning over a wretched pig,
for God's sake – this man, this *miracle*, had walked into his life.
In just 2 days' time, he could – he *would* – be rid of them all and have enough
money to provide him with the life of carefree luxury he deserved!

All he needed to do was evict Ida McGuirk…and therein lay a delicious
opportunity. Many years ago, when he was a young man, Colm had courted Ida
McGuirk, who was considered by many to be quite 'a catch'. The quiet and pretty
Ida had dreamed of meeting a Prince Charming but had only attracted the
attentions of a surly oaf – Colm. After a few months of 'stepping out' together,
Ida had informed Colm that henceforth they could only be friends and she saw
no future in a life together with him. An angry and hurt Colm had never forgiven
this slight and when fate delivered Ida to him years later as a *tenant*, he revelled
in every chance to make her life as uncomfortable as possible.

But now, with O'Meaney's eye-watering offer on the table, Colm saw his chance
at last to make Ida McGuirk *truly* regret the day she had turned him down!

But there was a teensy problem to deal with first: he was obliged to give the old
witch notice, which legally meant she could delay her departure for a month –
possibly even *longer*. Colm didn't have that kind of time. There was only one
thing for it. A bribe. If he was going to make half a *million*, then he felt sure that
he could spare a few *hundred* Euros to make her foolish old eyes light-up?

Half an hour later, Colm was sizing himself up in front of his faded bedroom mirror
– the one that he'd inherited from his long-dead Ma. He'd crammed into his only
half-decent suit and with his hair wet down, he felt confident he cut a dashing figure.

By the time he was striding boldly up Mrs McGuirk's – or rather *his* – tree-lined
driveway, clutching a slightly faded bunch of flowers he'd swiped from the local
graveyard, Colm was sweating profusely, and his distinctly old-fashioned suit
was cutting him under the armpits and around the waist. 'No bother', he thought
to himself, 'when I'm *rolling* in it, I'll be getting measured for the finest suits –
dozens of them – in Drogheda…or even in Dublin!'.

After a vigorous couple of knocks on Mrs McGuirk's front door, Colm attempted to puff himself up into what he hoped was a serious and dignified-looking posture. Finally, the front door creaked open.

"Ahhhh, Ida! How *lovely* to see you – you're looking the *picture* of good health and, may I say, fragrant loveliness! And who's this fine fellow with you?"

"Aidan…." said Aidan.
"Well, I had no idea Ida was blessed with such a – "
"Mr Quigley", said Mrs McGuirk. "…we're not used to visits from you.
It must be what – 10 years since you last called-by. The roof is *still* leaking, and toilet cistern *still* makes that funny clanking sound. Have you finally come to carry out the repairs?"
"Ah, ha ha…no, not exactly Ida…ha ha, er I've come about something else entirely. Something that I feel certain you're going to be very pleased to hear, *indeed*."
"Is that *so*? Well, I'll be the judge of that. I suppose you had better come in".

It wasn't the start he'd hoped for, Colm thought as he followed Mrs McGuirk and Aidan into the kitchen. As she started making a cup of tea for them both and found a vase for the stolen flowers, he reflected that this was a much nicer house than he remembered and that he really should have been charging the old woman at least three times what she was currently paying. Finally, with (he had to admit) a rather delicious cup of tea in hand, Colm cleared his throat and began:

"Ida – Mrs McGuirk – this is a day of celebration. I come to you with terrific news which, I feel sure, will change your life for the better in a *thousand* ways!"
Mrs McGuirk stared blankly back; no emotion evident on her kindly, old face.
Colm was about to continue, when the kitchen door creaked open and Paddy sauntered in and took up position next to Mrs McGuirk & Aidan, from where he too directed a similarly blank gaze towards the now somewhat agitated landlord.

"As I was, er, saying; Ida, I find myself in the happy position to offer you a sum of money that will utterly change your life for the better…er, in cash and, if you like, today!"
A grin frozen on his face; Colm waited on tenterhooks for Mrs McGuirk's response …everything hinged on it.

"Why?"
"Why, what?"
"Why have you turned up here after 10 years of total indifference towards me and this lovely old house in that ridiculous suit to offer me money?
What do you *want*, Colm Quigley?"

"Want? Oh, ha ha ha…yes, I see that this must look strange, but I'm only thinking of *your* happiness, Ida. I see that I've not been the best landlord and I'd like to make it up to you…and give you *€100*. Today. How does *that* sound?"

Mrs McGuirk seemed about to say something, when she and Paddy turned and looked at each other for a moment, as if reading each other's thoughts. Then, turning back towards Quigley:

"And what, exactly, do you expect in return? I'm no fool, Colm Quigley – there's nothing for nothing in this world".
"Return? Oh, ha – well, yes there is a little thing; I need you to move out this Friday. That is, the day after tomorrow."

At first, Colm couldn't be sure whether anyone had heard him. Mrs McGuirk didn't move, blink even. Aidan just stared…The pig too, was like a statue. There was just the drip of the kitchen sink tap...but as the seconds ticked by, the more fearful Colm became of what might be brewing. At last, his own nerves got the better of him:

"Perhaps I could stretch to €150......?"

"How *dare* you!", Mrs McGuirk suddenly exploded. "How DARE you come here after all these years and insult me like this! You maggot, you worm – get out! GET OUT or you'll know all about it!!!!!"

Mrs McGuirk was on her feet, as Colm was staggering to his.

"Have it your way, Ida! I plan to have *my* property back, with or *without* you accepting my extremely generous offer!!"

He started backing his way towards the front door as the old lady continued to bombard him with the kind of language he'd no idea little old ladies knew:

"This is my home, you weasel – where I live and have made a life, even though you've never spent a penny on the place, you miser! A home where I've raised animals and grown crops and cared for every living thing here with these hands – all without asking for a thing from you or anyone else!! I'm leaving here in a wooden box – and not a day before, as God is my witness. Now get **OUT**!!!!"

And with that final flourish, the front door slammed in Colm's face, leaving him shell-shocked on the porch.

And as he crunched his way angrily down the gravel drive, he muttered to himself:

"I tried to be nice – and *look* what I get in return? The woman's mad. €150!?!
I'm going to get her out, come what may. The day anyone – in particular a little old lady with her stupid pig - gets the better of Colm Quigley, is *the day pigs will fly*!"

CHAPTER 8
Paddy's Plea For Help

As Quigley's footsteps could be heard disappearing, Mrs McGuirk was left standing in her hallway feeling like she never had before: utterly helpless, grief-stricken, and alone. Tears welled-up in her eyes and, as she sank onto the stairs, she couldn't prevent the sobs as they came thick and fast from somewhere deep inside her. As silently as he could, Aidan put his arms around her neck… and Paddy gently pushed his wet nose onto her shaking lap:

"Oh Aidan – *Paddy*!!! Whatever am I to do? I never dreamed that anybody – even that wretch Quigley – would ever ask me to leave my lovely home. I've been alone here all these years, but I have never once been lonely – not until this very minute….".
"Please don't cry Granny – *please*? We have 'til Friday – I'm sure we can come up with some way to stop Quigley before then…I'll think of something, I promise", mumbled Aidan, also struggling to hold back his tears…

But even as he whispered these words to a now inconsolable Mrs McGuirk, Aidan struggled to believe them himself. 'Colm Quigley owns this house', he thought, 'and he probably *can* throw us out – if not Friday, then soon. I need some help…someone who knows about these things and –', Aidan stopped mid-thought: of course; he knew someone who could help!

* * *

After Aidan had finally convinced Mrs McGuirk to stop crying and instead go upstairs for a much-needed nap, he lifted the latch on the back door and, beckoning Paddy to follow him, closed it gently behind him, the pair shuffled out through the garden and off down the field. The other animals on the farm were already used to Paddy trotting around the place – sometimes practicing talking to himself and, every now and then, flying a few quick circuits to keep in shape - sort of like a teenager rehearsing dance moves on front of their bedroom mirror. But they'd never seen Paddy & Aidan out strolling *together*….

Paddy was in no position to stop for a chat with Molly, the old mare – or any of the cows who, in any case, seemed consumed with consuming – grass, for the most part.

As they made their way down the field, Paddy began to have an uncomfortable feeling; why was Aidan heading in this direction…and with what seemed to Paddy a more *determined* step than usual? So determined, in fact, that Paddy was slightly struggling to keep up. Suddenly:

"We could do with a drop of rain Paddy, wouldn't you say?"
Paddy was so startled by Aidan's question that it took every ounce of self-control to avoid answering…. but Aidan continued:

"Quigley is a terrible man – how can we ever stop him?"

Again – Paddy just about stuck to his guns and managed to keep his trap shut.

"I mean," Aidan pressed on, "if *we* don't do something – who will?"

By now, Paddy was at his wits' end. He'd made a solemn promise to the King of the Fairies to *never* breathe a word to anyone except Mrs McGuirk about the little people and his own magic powers. Despite the nagging sense that Aidan suspected *something*, Paddy felt confident that no-one – and certainly not a young boy – was going to outsmart a pig with his magical powers!

"Watch out, Paddy – you'll step on that nail!", Aidan suddenly blurted out.
"What nail? Where?? I can't see….a…………………..nail".

As these last syllables of Paddy's drifted away on the breeze, Paddy and Aidan were left staring at each other, standing stock still, breathing through their mouths…

Like a stand-off in one of the old black and white Westerns Mrs McGuirk loved to watch sometimes, there was a tense wait to see who would make the next move…

"……so, it's true. you can *speak*!?"
"I'm not saying another word". said Paddy, saying another 5 words.
"How? How is it possible that you can speak – you're a pig!!"

Paddy stared back – now with his jaws clamped shut. But perhaps realizing that this was a case of shutting the stable door after the horse – or in this case pig – had bolted, his determination seemed to suddenly desert him.

"I rescued the king of the fairies…he granted me some wishes…so I can talk and, er….fly".

"Fly?!?! *FLY*?!?!?!?! you mean like a *bird* flies?"

"Well, no…. sort of, yes…. a bit, I mean. I'm not supposed to tell anyone except Mrs McGuirk – I promised. And now you've made me tell *you*….".

After saying these words, Paddy looked so utterly dejected and miserable, standing there with his head drooping and his eyes downcast, that Aidan was overcome with shame that he'd forced dear old Paddy to break a promise to someone. Especially as that someone was none other than the King of the Fairies.

"Look, Paddy – I'm sorry. I didn't mean to trick you, but I think the fairies would understand – don't you? Granny – Ida – is in danger. Quigley is up to no good and you and she could lose your home unless we come up with a way to stop him! You want to keep your home, don't you?"
"Yes, of course…but what can *I* do? For a start, I'm a pig – and not many people listen to pigs – and also if people knew about my magic powers, Mrs McGuirk says I'd be put in a circus!"

Paddy was right. Aidan knew that although most of the inhabitants of Termonfeckin were grand people who treated Paddy as one of their own, one or two of them might *not* react well to finding themselves playing second fiddle to a talking and flying pig.

For a moment, both boy and pig were silent, engulfed in their own thoughts and the sounds of a beautiful Irish summer's day…

But sometimes, just a moment's silence can work miracles.

"Paddy – I think I know what we must do!"
"You do?", said a relieved-looking Paddy.
"You must go and see the fairies and tell them what's happened – and ask them to help us. Maybe they'll have an idea?"

"But the king told me that fairies can *never* interfere in the world of humans – if they did, they'd put themselves in mortal danger".

"Then you must tell them that if Quigley gets his way, they could be in a lot more danger than they've *ever* faced before! And don't – I repeat don't – tell them that *I* know your secret".

"But that's being dishonest, isn't it?", mumbled Paddy.

"Only a teensy-weensy bit…. after all, you didn't choose to tell me – I tricked you, didn't I?"

And before Paddy had a chance to explore this undoubted moral conundrum further, Aidan broke in:

"Hurry up now, Paddy. Go and find this King of yours and tell him that we – I mean *you* – need his help. I'm going back to see if Granny's alright".

* * *

After 5 minutes, Paddy had reached the stream and got to work finding a fairy. Although it was the King he needed to speak to, Paddy thought it might be best to stick to formalities and be announced…

"Orla!? Orla! Are you there?" But there was only silence.
"Orla – *pleeeeeease*! I need to talk to you!..".

After a couple more attempts, after which he was going to have to try something more drastic, there was suddenly a response…

"Paddy?! What on earth are you doing here – especially this time of day?", said a very sleepy-looking Orla, as she pushed some twigs to one side.
"It's an emergency – I need to talk to the King".
"An emergency? Are you sure about that? This is the time of day we're all enjoying a much-needed nap – so this had *better* be important. Let's see: is it a matter of life or death?"
"Well, not exactly…",
"Has there been too much rain and we're going to be flooded?"
"No, I just need…",
"Is Christmas being cancelled?"
"No – look, please stop – I need to see the King, ***now***!"

Paddy realized that he had raised his voice and Orla was now looking at him – silent.

"Oh…right, well if you're *sure* it's important," she said, a little more patiently, "then I suppose I'd better go and wake His Majesty up…".

"Yes, please Orla…and I'm sorry I was shouting".
"You're forgiven, Paddy…I'll be back shortly".

Five very long minutes later, His Majesty was standing in front of Paddy,
rubbing his eyes and not looking at all happy.

"Paddy, correct me if I'm wrong, but you were given magical powers so that you
could solve problems – am I right?!"
"Yes, but I don't think I can solve this one alone."
"Oh, why not?"
"Because Colm Quigley has given Mrs McGuirk two days to pack up the house
and leave – and we have nowhere to go and she's very upset and I'm not sure
how to help her and she's crying lots
and – "….
"Alright Paddy – calm *down*!", interrupted the King.
"Tell me what's happened…".

So, for the next few minutes, Paddy relayed everything he knew about the farm, Mrs McGuirk, and Colm Quigley. The King, Orla and a few other fairies who had now woken-up and had come to see what all the fuss was about, listened quietly. Finally, when Paddy could think of nothing else to add, His Majesty cleared his throat and spoke:

"So, just to be clear. You're saying that Mrs McGuirk – and you – have been told to leave a house you don't own by the man who owns it?"
"Well, yes…".
"Which he is entitled to do?"
"Yes…I suppose so…".
"And he's offered Mrs McGuirk money as compensation?"
"€150…. I think".
"Hmmm…. let me think…".

After digesting Paddy's answers a little longer while stroking his beard, the King seemed to reach some sort of conclusion.

"Well Paddy, I'm not sure how we can help. Colm Quigley is a mean, spiteful man – that's true enough. But is he doing anything he's not allowed to? No, not really. And anyway, what would you have *us* do?'.

It was, thought Paddy, a good question: what *did* he want the Fairies to do? Aidan had said the King might have an idea, but what if he didn't? And even if he did – *why* would he want to risk the lives of all the fairies in his kingdom to help an old lady and a pig? But then, just as Paddy was beginning to think that this was all a waste of time, a little voice piped up:

"Colm Quigley is a bad, bad man. But why does he want your Mrs McGuirk to move out *suddenly*?" It was the tiniest of the little people, Seamo, who had spoken. "Money is the only thing that man has *ever* cared for – and it'll be money that's behind all this."
Paddy didn't know whether he was meant to say something or not.
So, he said nothing. Instead, the King stepped forward:

"Paddy, Seamo may be the smallest amongst us – but he's often the wisest. We need to know *why* Quigley wants to throw you and Mrs McGuirk out. And when we do, we'll decide what to do then. Agreed?"
"Agreed!" said Paddy, now feeling much happier than he did a few moments ago. And with that, he said his goodbyes and left the Fairies to their discussions.

CHAPTER 9
A Den Of Thieves

But while Paddy was down talking to the Fairies, Mrs McGuirk had managed to get a little sleep after being so horribly upset; and, as Aidan had predicted before he and Paddy had crept out of the house – it'd done her the world of good. After an hour or so, she woke up, called Paddy's name once or twice and after hearing no answer, padded downstairs to make herself a cup of tea, after which she thought the chickens probably needed feeding. To her delight, there was Aidan just pouring boiling water into her favourite tea pot.

"I thought you might need a cup of tea, Granny?"
"You read my mind – what a kind boy you are…your mother would have been very proud of you".

After just one sip out of her favourite china cup, Mrs McGuirk began to feel a *tiny* bit better. She was about to reach for one of her favourite shortcake biscuits – when she happened to glance out of the kitchen window. There was a man she'd never seen before in her back garden, holding what looked like a tape measure and a large map under his arm. Without thinking, she banged loudly on the window. Bold as brass, the man looked straight at her, doffed his Trilby and grinned a large toothy grin right back at her!

"Stay here, Aidan!"

Within seconds, Mrs McGuirk was outside, eyeball-to-eyeball with the stranger.

"You're trespassing!", she shouted at him. "Who are you?"
"Tom O'Meaney, at your service! You must be Mrs McGuirk? I understand you're moving out of here at the end of the week and, since *I* shall be moving in – I thought I'd get a good look at the place!"

"I'm going nowhere, young fella, so you can wipe that supercilious smirk off your kisser straight away".

"Instead of threatening me, you'd be better off packing some suitcases, old woman. Don't worry, I was leaving anyhow – I've seen enough of my new property for now. Plenty of time to see more after Friday! Toodle pip!!"

And with that, he tipped his hat again and whistling jauntily – disappeared, leaving poor Mrs McGuirk, with her arms hanging limply by her sides and wishing for all the world that the earth would swallow her up and end her misery that very moment.

* * *

"*Jayyyyyysus*, Quigley – you should have seen the look on her poor auld face!!! It was enough to make me believe in Fairies – *hahahahahahaha*!!!!"

A mere 10 minutes after leaving Mrs McGuirk bereft in her back garden, Tom O'Meaney was already draining the last few drops of his Guinness, just poured by an oily and anxious Colm Quigley.

"Honest to God Quigley, am I glad I met *you* – the farm is *perfect*! I'll have to knock down the house and the hay barn, of course and I'll want to get rid of that gravel driveway with all those pine trees – just a straight concrete service road so that the meat trucks can drive straight into the loading bays would be best…".
"Whatever you want, Mr O'Meaney – it'll be yours to do as you wish with it by Friday afternoon. Talking of which, er, you mentioned half a *million*….".

And as the two men huddled down to talk hard cash, they didn't notice that 10 feet above their heads, listening and watching ever so quietly – were Seamo and Orla – peering down through a skylight at the den of thieves below.

***

After leaving the fairies to (hopefully) devise a plan of action, Paddy trudged back up the field for his supper, wishing he had better news to share with Mrs McGuirk. But at least he wasn't coming home with bad news.

As he closed the back door of the house behind him, Paddy thought he could hear a strange noise coming from the kitchen. Stopping outside the door, he soon realized what it was.

There, next to the fire, was Aidan with his arms around his Granny's neck. Poor Mrs McGuirk was sobbing quietly…. the sleep didn't seem to have done her any good at all. She looked up and saw Paddy standing quietly by the door:

Seemingly unconscious that she was addressing a pig, she said:

"An awful man was here, Paddy – wearing a grin and a dreadful hat. He says he's the new owner!
Are we really going to lose our home?!"
Aidan quickly cut in: "Now come along, Granny – don't cry. I told you I would find a way to solve this – and I will. In fact, just a little earlier I – "…

Bang, bang, bang!!!

Ida, Aidan and Paddy all jumped. Someone was giving the front door a good hammering.

Bang, bang!!

"Oh goodness…whatever now – I'm not sure I can take another visit from anyone else horrible today", said Mrs McGuirk, as she shuffled, anxiously down the hallway. But there, standing at the front door was, to all intents and purposes, another horrible man. This one was also wearing a trilby along with an ill-fitting rain mac and was carrying a battered, brown leather briefcase.

"Yes?"
"My name is Fitzgerald – I've come to talk to you, Mrs McGuirk – and see if we can't sort out this terrible misunderstanding?
"Misunderstanding?"

"Yes. I'm a solicitor from *Fitzgerald & Shelby's*. My client, Mr Quigley is not a sophisticated man, you understand, and I fear he may have got off on the wrong foot with you. May I come in?"

And before Mrs McGuirk could utter a word, Fitzgerald was already half-way to the kitchen.

"Aidan", said Mrs McGuirk, "be a good boy and go and wait with Paddy in the sitting room".

Barely drawing breath, the unctuous solicitor continued:

"Lovely place you have here. I quite see why you're so attached to it. Now, let me explain why I'm here", Fitzgerald breezily continued. "My client, Mr C Quigley wishes to re-acquire this property by this Friday – and is, naturally, prepared to make you a *very* generous offer to compensate you for any *inconvenience* this may cause you".

"*Inconvenience*!? Now look *here*, I – ", attempted Mrs McGuirk.

"All in good time, all in good time", interrupted Fitzgerald, "…now what sort of money are we talking about here? €200? €250? I could see if my client would be prepared to stretch to *€500*, perhaps? No *promises*, of course…."

"I don't want any money from you – or Quigley – or anyone else, thank you ever so much. And what's more, you can take your – ".

"Yes, yes – ", Fitzgerald cut in, "…Mr Quigley said you'd say that. He also said that you were a completely unreasonable woman, and no amount of money would make you see sense…and I have to say, I'm beginning to see what he meant! Now, here's a document I'd like to get your signature on".

Mrs McGuirk was about to explode in a rage, the likes of which neither Fitzgerald - nor Termonfeckin had ever witnessed before – when the kitchen door creaked open. Both she, and the ghastly Fitzgerald fellow turned their heads towards the noise.

And there, standing innocently, was Paddy – dressed in a pair of Mrs McGuirk's bloomers, one of her old brassieres covering his ears and a slightly chewed pair of yellow, children's sunglasses perched awkwardly on his snout – while Aidan stood next to him in an old pinafore, over-sized wellingtons, and a bee-keepers hat.

Fitzgerald looked, for all the world, as though he'd been turned to stone. Paddy, grunting, shuffled up as close as he could get to him:

"Mr Fitzgerald – we'd be *much* obliged if you'd leave us alone. Please".

It was lucky that Mrs McGuirk had no neighbours within earshot, as the screams would have brought them all running. Fitzgerald was out the front door in a flash, his shouts could be heard all the way down the driveway.

"You forgot your hat!", shouted Mrs McGuirk, after the retreating figure.
"*And* your briefcase!", cried Aidan.

A minute later, with the front door closed, all three of them were crying with laughter. It was the first time happiness had filled the house for what seemed like days.

"That was *very* naughty of you, Paddy – do you mean to tell me that Aidan knows your secret - I thought we agreed you'd never talk in front of people?"
"I know I did, Mrs McGuirk – but it seems Aidan already knew…and no-one will believe Fitz-whatever his name was, and he'll never dare come back here. And anyway, you've suffered enough for one day. Let's put the kettle on and try and think what to do next, shall we?"

CHAPTER 10
The Kidnap

"Calm down, caaaaalm down Fitzgerald – you're making no sense at all!"

Colm Quigley was pouring the third straight whiskey – not the expensive stuff – for the grown man now blubbering in front of him.

"Just tell me - did she sign the document or not?"

"I don't know…there…there was a *pig*! In *sunglasses* for God's sake!! It asked me to *leave*!! What kind of business have you got me mixed up in here Quigley?!"

"There, there, Fitz – you've been working too hard lately. Don't worry yourself, I won't make you go back there".

By now, Quigley was certain he'd made a huge mistake in hiring Fitzgerald. The poor man was delusional and what was worse, his snivelling was upsetting some of the other customers.

"Why don't you go home and have a little lie-down, Fitz?", Colm hissed in an urgent whisper.
"Do you think I should, Quigley?"
"Absolutely. I'll take care of the old lady. Off you go, now".

And with that, Colm ushered a tipsy Fitzgerald out of the pub, closing the door quietly behind him.
But all the while the solicitor had been jabbering at him, an idea had been slowly taking shape in his head: this pig of Mrs McGuirk's was plainly making life difficult. Of *course*, he couldn't *talk* – but just the same, the old bat was very fond of him…. *very* fond, in fact….

* * *

No more than an hour had passed since the incident described above. Colm, fearful that Fitzgerald's visit to Mrs McGuirk's had only made matters worse, decided to take matters firmly in hand. His own hand. He was now parked as discreetly as possible in his battered, ex-Post Office van a short distance from the entrance to Mrs McGuirk's driveway. The rear doors were open, and an old plank was propped up against the rear sill – as though ready for a wheelbarrow to be pushed up it. Colm was ready for a long wait and had brought a flask full of tea with some of his favourite biscuits to help make the clock tick faster.

The only person who came into view was old Noggin, who clattered past with his mule and flatbed cart. He'd already had a few in Quigley's Bar and was almost certainly too tipsy to notice anything much.

And it looked as if the fates were smiling on Colm; if he wasn't mistaken, after only one gulp of tea, he could just make out what sounded like the contented grunting and scoffing sounds of that wretchedly annoying pig…

Amazingly, Colm's plan was going…well, according to plan. The trail of Salt 'n Vinegar crisps he'd strewn the length of Mrs McGuirk's driveway was enough to lure the greedy porker straight into Colm's arms. Within another couple of nail-biting minutes, Paddy was now standing, somewhat unsteadily, surveying the trail of crisps leading up the gangplank and into the back of the van.

For Paddy, after what had been a *terrible* day and no lunch, finding a trail of free, delicious snacks like this was a heaven-sent diversion guaranteed to lift the spirits and restore morale. Oddly though, he was suddenly feeling incredibly tired and could happily enjoy a lie-down under a hedge somewhere. But that would mean *not* enjoying the remaining crisps that lay in front of him – and, quite possibly, *inside* the van. With one heroic grunt, he pushed himself up the ramp…hoovering crisps as he went, until he found himself inside.

"Perhaps, if I just have a little rest here for a minute or two, I'll get a second wind….and finish off…. the last of….".

Paddy was already snoring as an ecstatic Quigley *slammed* the rear doors shut, jumped into the driver's seat, and roared off down the road – hooting with joy as he did so:

"Gotcha !! My piggly-wiggly pal – you greedy *get*! Naughty old Uncle Colm sprinkled every one of those crisps with sleeping pills – and you swallowed the *lot*! Sweet dreams, my snoring, porky prisoner – hahahaha!!"

* * *

Under ordinary circumstances, despite consuming a large quantity of Tayto crisps – Paddy would have no real trouble in polishing-off whatever Mrs McGuirk had prepared for his dinner as well. And since it was now around supper time, and even though making some food for Paddy was the last thing she felt like doing, she dutifully filled his bowl with some carrots, potato peelings, oats and some honey – as a treat. But Paddy didn't appear at his usual time, 6'o clock. Or at 6.30….or at 7'o clock, either. A couple of times, she sent Aidan outside, banging the pan that usually brought him running – but of Paddy, there was no sign.

Thinking back, she now realized that the last time she had set eyes on him was as they watched Fitzgerald disappear, shrieking, off down the driveway.

"Oh Paddy," she quietly cried to herself as she got herself ready for bed. "Where *are* you? I need you here, especially this evening – it's been the *worst* day of my life and only *you* can cheer me up…".

But no matter how many *Hail Mary's* a tearful Mrs McGuirk said before climbing into bed, it made no difference: Paddy was gone – and poor Mrs McGuirk had no *idea* where.

CHAPTER 11
Quigley's Bar

But while Mrs McGuirk had the *worst* night's sleep after the worst day of her life – Colm Quigley had the *best* night's sleep he could remember. He'd managed to get that dimwit pig out of the way and that daft old woman just where he wanted her – scared and soon ready to do anything she was told!

In the best mood he'd been in for ages, Colm ate a hearty breakfast – one slice of un-buttered toast and a boiled egg – slammed his front door shut, secured his bicycle clips around his ankles, and peddled happily back to the village and his soon-to-be-forgotten pub.

Once inside the deserted saloon bar, Colm listened intently for any noises. Nothing. Creeping behind the bar, he unbolted the trapdoor there and cautiously lifted it a couple of inches. And there, staring mutely up at him was Paddy.

"Good morning pig! Hope you had a *restful* night? Just so we understand one another – if your precious Mrs McGuirk doesn't sign that document, then *you're* for the chop! In fact, you'll be turned into a shop-full of pork chops at the new sausage factory – and that's a *promise*! Hahahaha!!!"

Colm let the trapdoor crash shut and whistling, got on with getting ready for opening time at 12.

Back at home, a very worried Mrs McGuirk could do no more than fiddle with her rosary beads next to the unlit parlour fire as she watched Aidan push his uneaten breakfast around his plate. She hadn't eaten breakfast either and wasn't in any sort of mood to try.

Just then, the letterbox clanged loudly, and something dropped onto the doormat. Mrs McGuirk hardly ever received mail, so hurried into the hallway. As the crunch of the postman's shoes died away, she picked up the envelope lying there – and tore it open. On a single sheet of white paper, spelled out in letters cut from a newspaper:

'IF YEW WANT TO SEE YOR PRESHUS PET AGAIN –
YEW NO WOT TO DO'.

if YEW wanT tO SEE yoR pREshuS PeT agAIn – YewnO woT To Do

At first, Mrs McGuirk couldn't make head or tail of what the message meant. But after Aidan read it aloud a couple of times, it suddenly made sense. But before she could gather her thoughts, a voice behind them piped-up:

"Don't worry about Paddy, missus – he's big enough and ugly enough to look after himself. I promise you we'll find him".

* * *

At 12 sharp, a whistling Colm Quigley pulled back the bolts on the pub door to reveal his first customer already waiting. And, as usual, he knew who it would be: Noggin, the itinerant potato seller, who could easily be mistaken for a tramp.

"Morning Noggin, how the devil are you today?"

This was a question Noggin was rarely asked and certainly never by Quigley. Ordinarily, as soon as the door was open, Noggin pushed straight past Colm without a word and waited patiently while his first pint of Guinness was being poured by the landlord. No one in the village knew Noggin's real name, or exactly where he lived – only that a caravan was involved and, incredibly, that he was married. And not to his mule. He was used to being ignored – and returned the compliment with interest. Noggin earned his living by selling spuds around Termonfeckin and a couple of other nearby villages. They sat in a pile on the flat bed cart his mule, 'Nancy', pulled behind her, with Noggin sitting up top and occasionally shouting 'Balls of flour!! Balls of flooooooour….", the best description he could think of for the 3rd rate produce he spent his days collecting and selling. Any un-sold potatoes at the end of each week were soon used, in Noggin's home-made distillery next to his caravan, where he created the finest 'pocheen' in all-Ireland. The resulting alcohol was so powerful that only Noggin and his wife could drink it. After years of doing so, both were red-faced, had noses like cauliflowers and were often described as being 'away with the fairies', by many of his customers.

But enough about Noggin – for now.

In the next 10 minutes or so, the bar slowly filled up – 4 or 5 regulars at first, then – as it was market day in nearby Drogheda – scores of noisy farmers either lamenting the losses they'd made on their sales or celebrating having 'got one over' on one of the former. In any event, today was a big money day for the farmers – *and* Colm, who was pouring pints as if his life depended on it. Which, in a way, it did.

But while all was noisy hubbub upstairs, down below it was a *very* different story. In his damp prison cell, the only company a very sad pig had was the occasional muffled laughter and shouts filtering down to him, besides which the only other sounds were the hisses & gurgles of pipes, barrels & tubes to keep him company.

"No one knows I'm here. Not a *soul*. Poor Mrs McGuirk and Aidan must be worried sick…. all of this will be the death of her. And even *with* all my magical powers, there's not a thing I can do stuck in here…

But just at that very moment, Paddy had a brainstorm: if I can hear them up *there* – then they must be able to hear *me* down *here*?

At the sound of a little, unfamiliar voice behind them – Mrs McGuirk nearly jumped out of her skin and let out an *almighty* shriek. She whipped around to face whatever demon had snuck into her house – only to be confronted with a tiny little *man* sitting on the end of the bannisters, looking for all the world as if he owned the place.

"I'm Seamus, missus – but you can call me 'Seamo'."

When Paddy first told her about rescuing the King of the Fairies and being granted magic wishes, Mrs McGuirk wasn't *entirely* sure whether to totally believe what she heard. Aidan too had only *just* believed Paddy because he could talk. Now, with a little man calling himself 'Seamo' no bigger than her own – not very big – hand, neither of them had much choice. There really were fairies…and here was one!

Mrs McGuirk realized that she had better say something…

"Well, er…'hello', Seamo. How are you?"
"I'm grand, *meself*, thanks – but I'd say, by the look of you, that you're not".
"No…. I suppose, I'm not….in fact, I'm……………*boo hoo hooooooooooooooooooooo*".

Poor Mrs McGuirk stood in the hallway, bawling her eyes out. Seamo had to almost shout to get himself heard:

"Calm yerself, Ida – *caaaaalm* yerself! I've a pretty good idea who's behind all this – and so do you".

With these words, Mrs McGuirk's crying suddenly reduced to just sniffling.

"What do you mean?"
"Who's been making your life *hell* this past day? Who's mean, greedy and stupid enough to try *anything*?
"Colm Quigley …."
"And who else in Termonfeckin would have any reason to want Paddy out of the way?"
"I, er….no-one?"
"Dat's right – no-one. Once Colm Quigley has got you out, he's planning to sell the land to that man O'Meaney. He's going to build a sausage factory!"

57

Mrs McGuirk's jaw dropped, while Aidan's eyes suddenly filled with tears and the blackmail letter fluttered from his hand….

"A what? You mean…. you mean…."
"Yes", chipped in Seamo, "turn harmless animals like Paddy into sausages – and pork chops…and bacon…and pork scratchings…and fashionable shoes and designer handbags and – "
"That's enough, Seamo! This is awful…. just awful….".

And just as it looked as though Mrs McGuirk was about to start welling up again, Seamo cut in:

"Colm Quigley has Paddy a prisoner somewhere – nothing else makes sense. Who do you think has sent you that note you were holding? If you sign over the house and land – you'll get Paddy back…. maybe".

But the fairies in Ireland know a thing or two about making the best of things - and how to deal with bad men. After all, if they didn't, how would they still be here today?

"Do you promise me there'll be no more tears, Mrs McGuirk?"
"Yes…".
"And do you promise to believe me when I tell you that if you listen to me, not only will we find Paddy, but we'll make Colm Quigley wish he'd never picked on a little old lady or messed with the people and fairies of Termonfeckin?!"
"Yes, I do!", answered a suddenly smiling Mrs McGuirk and Aidan in unison.
"Good – then let's get to work!"

* * *

"So, what should I do?", thought Paddy to himself.
"A pig shouting 'Help!' – that might work….".

But for reasons he was at a loss to explain to himself, something else *entirely* popped into his head.
Quietly, at first, Paddy began to sing:

'*There was a man called Michael Finnegan, he grew whiskers on his chinegan…the wind came up and blew them in-again, poor old Michael Finnegan – begin-again….*'

And the more he sang, the *better* he started to feel – and the *louder* his voice started to get.

By now, one or two of the less-sozzled drinkers had stopped gassing and started to prick up their ears. Not understanding exactly what it was they were hearing, there were a couple of clever-dick remarks:

"Jaysus, Quigley – we always thought you were too *mean* to put a jukebox in here!"
"Who've you got down there, Colm – *Elvis*?!"
"Whoever he is – he's a grand set of pipes on him, Quigley – you should give him a regular guest spot. Hahahaha!"

To Colm's growing horror, the bar started to quieten down to listen, as a fruity baritone filtered upwards through the floorboards…

'…. *ran a race and thought he'd win again, got so puffed that he had to go in-again – poor old Michael Finnegan….begin-again*!

By now, Colm had a sickly grin spread across his face; paralyzed with a thousand competing and nightmarish thoughts crashing through his brain, he stood rooted to the spot with a tea towel and empty glass suspended limply in his hands.

But as if baby Jesus himself was looking out for Colm, a miracle occurred: *Noggin*, quiet 'til now, started to sing along with the mystery vocalist….

'…*he grew fat and then grew thin again, then he died and had to begin again….*'

And the rest of the pub, unable to resist a rousing chorus of a much-loved song – joined in with gusto:

'...*poor old Michael Finnegan*....***begin again***!!!!!'

As the last words rang out, the entire pub – nearly all farmers – erupted into cheering and laughing and a chorus of fresh orders at the bar for refills.

Colm was saved.

Poor Paddy.

All hope gone; he sank to the floor to await his fate.

But one man sat quietly, ignored as usual…. finished his drink and slipped unnoticed out of the bar.

CHAPTER 12
The Rescue

At 3pm sharp, a much perkier Colm Quigley shoved the last of his drunker customers out and hastily bolted the door behind them.

He slumped against it, a wave of relief washing over him…along with a tingling sensation that told him that *something* wasn't right – only Paddy is down in the cellar. So, *who* was singing? Colm's imagination was on fire.

It was time to find out.

He tentatively slid the bolts on the trapdoor and lifted it open a few inches. A forlorn-looking Paddy was staring back at him. Not a sign of anyone else:

"Just one more night for you down here, my porky pal – if I don't have a signed agreement in my hands by midday tomorrow, then tonight will be your last on Earth! Hahahahahhhaa!!!!!"

Colm had no sooner stopped laughing, than he had to remind himself that he was on his hands and knees, talking to a pig through a trapdoor.

"What's the matter with me? I'm becoming as much of an *eejit* as this dumb beast in front of me!"

But no sooner had this thought entered – and then left his brain, than for the second time in a day, Colm's entire universe imploded:

"*There was a man called Michael Finnegan, he grew whiskers on his chinegan…the wind came up and blew them inagain, poor old Michael Finnegan – beginagain*!", sang Paddy.

In the slack-jawed silence that followed, Colm's dentures snapped shut of their own accord, leaving them on display inside his open, gawping gob. The only noise was the gentle drip of the pipes in the cellar.

Then Colm started howling – a noise difficult to describe unless you were there. A bewildered shrieking - crossed with a plaintive *wail*. He crashed the trapdoor down, his fingers desperately fumbling to lock it, all the while making this terrible noise.

He stood bolt upright, backing away into the bottles and empty glasses lining the bar, hardly able to tear his eyes away from the now-shut trapdoor. Grabbing the nearest bottle with anything in it, and with shaking hands, he gulped down its entire contents. No two thoughts were forming themselves into any other larger thought – Colm's mind was on *fire* – ablaze with colliding images and words…. when he was interrupted by a voice from the bowels of his hated bar:

"You're a wicked and *terrible* man, Colm Quigley – and you'll never, *ever* get away with this!"

But despite the state he was in, some part of Colm's brain was still functioning - and he found himself suddenly outraged that he feared a talking pig:

"Er, ha! Do you really think that a *pig* – even one that sings and speaks – and a daft old woman are going to get in the way of the biggest business deal that Termonfeckin has ever seen??! never…*ever*!!!!!!"

* * *

Although Colm Quigley had made a lot of money over the 30+ years he'd been the owner and landlord of the pub of the same name, he was a mean man, never spending more than was necessary while despising those he thought frivolous and spendthrifts. The interior of his pub looked the same as it did the day he opened for business all those years ago. Although he sometimes slept in a rough simple bed in the attic above the pub if he was too tired (or a little the worse for wear) – he much preferred to cycle the 10 minutes to his rather plain cottage down on the Baltray Road. This was most definitely one of those evenings. Wild horses couldn't keep him close to the pub tonight, not with a spiteful, singing pig locked in the cellar.

After double-checking that every bolt and lock was securely fastened, he slapped a 'Closed 'til Further Notice' sign on the front door – leapt onto his rickety old bike and pedalled off home as fast as he could. His route took him past one of the two graveyards in Termonfeckin. Normally, the slumbering dead were of no interest to him whatsoever – Colm only ever affected a religious air if it helped him make money – but tonight he pedalled past the shadowed tombstones as though his life depended on it. 7'34" seconds later he was panting and sweating *like* a pig inside his own silent hallway and double locking his front door. As he tried to control his breathing, he began to slowly get his thoughts in order: 'Could it really be true that a pig had threatened him? And where had he learned the lyrics to *Michael Finnegan*, for God's sake?!'. Colm realized that if he didn't get a grip of himself *toute de suite*, not only would the deal of a lifetime slip through his fingers – but maybe even everything he'd ever worked for! All the pleasures he had denied himself – fancy clothes, a swanky car, a grand house and worst of all, a glamorous and admiring wife to adore him and care for him – all those sacrifices would have been for *nothing*, if Mrs Ida McGuirk didn't sign that agreement by tomorrow at midday.

As he trudged up the bare wooden staircase, he consoled himself with the thought that a good night's sleep – a better one than that awful pig, at least – would make everything better by the morning and by then, Colm would know *exactly* what to do. He dropped his yellowing dentures into a glass of murky water next to his bed, shuffled clumsily into his faded and slightly stained pyjamas and climbed, groaning and grateful beneath the one blanket he kept on his bed.

With only the occasional *gurgle, fpop!* and *drip* from the pipes and barrels around him, Paddy was at the lowest of low ebbs. What good were his special powers now, when all Quigley had to do was lock him in a cellar to keep him under control? He might as well just be the pig he once was, happily dozing the days away and being nagged by Mrs McGuirk – how blissful all that seemed now…. Somehow, Paddy felt, this was *all* his fault.

Just then, he thought he heard something. A scraping metal sound just above him…followed by a sharp 'clang!'. A beam of light hit Paddy straight in the eyes. Fearing that it must be Quigley, returning to do something terrible to him, Paddy instinctively backed away into the corner of the cellar.

"Paddy? Are you down there? *Paddy* – are you alright?"

A wave of *relief* swept over Paddy. Staring down at him was Aidan, Mrs McGuirk and a twinkling *swarm* of fairies!

"He's alive – he's alright – he's grand!", they chorused.

In a trice, Paddy had flown up through the open trapdoor, knocking a beaming Mrs McGuirk over in the process.

"Oh, Padddy – Paddy!! You're alive, you're *alive*!!!We've been worried sick about you. You're not *hurt*, are you?"

'Not a *bother* on me, Mrs McGuirk, I'm fine, so I am…but how did you know where to find me?

"It's a long story…but it turns out that Noggin sometimes sells a little of his 'produce' to the fairies…who said they were searching for you and that Quigley must be involved…and Noggin worked out that it could only be you locked in this cellar!"

Paddy realized that now was not the moment to dwell on the revelation that Noggin, of all people, was his saviour: "Listen, Ida - I don't think we have very long! Quigley is determined to get you to sign over everything – the house, the farm – by midday tomorrow. And if you won't sign, I'm sure he'll do something *terrible* to you both – and especially me".

But before Mrs McGuirk could respond, a different voice piped-up, one Paddy had heard once before:

"Colm Quigley is a mean, lying maggot – and he needs teaching a lesson he *won't* forget!"

The voice belonged to Seamo.

"But I don't intend to sign *any* piece of paper – he can't *make* me", said Mrs McGuirk.

"He won't have to – he's a rogue, he'll find a way, believe me. He'd cheat the Pope if he got the chance – that's the kind of man he is."

"Seamo's right,' said Aidan. "We need to hit Quigley where it hurts – he needs to look like the last man on earth *anyone* – even Tom O'Meaney – would *ever* do business with".

It was at this point that Paddy, who had been listening carefully to everything that had been said, chose to speak:

"I *think* I have an idea…but it will need all of us to work together…and there isn't a *moment* to lose".

* * *

CHAPTER 13

Paddy The Banshee

Getting to sleep, normally so easy for Colm, who found just counting money in his head would do the trick had, for the first time in a long time, lain wide awake for well over an hour trying – and failing – to make sense of the scarcely believable events of the previous few days. But with adrenaline & whiskey still coursing through his veins, it took a heroic effort to finally drift off into a fitful slumber…

The first thing that Colm next became semi-aware of was that he was cold… and in his half-asleep state was unable to pull his one sheet back over himself.

Because it wasn't there.

Assuming he had kicked it onto the floor, he groggily opened one eye, hoping to find his beloved *blanky* and snuggle back down under it – and back to sleep. Instead, his blanky was dancing in the air in front of his face. With a shriek, he sat bolt upright and tried to shuffle backwards into the furthest corner of his rickety old bed.

At the exact same moment, the room suddenly filled with light.

Hundreds of tiny lights were dancing inside the sheet like swarm of fireflies. Colm's eyes bulged wide in terror and disbelief, his toothless jaw slack and quivering as though he was about to cry. Just then a voice boomed out:

"Colm Quigley – you are not dreaming. Listen *very* carefully: if you make any further attempt to force Mrs McGuirk from her home, I will come to visit you every night & make sure you never sleep another wink ever again".

Colm remained speechless and transfixed.

But despite the sheer impossibility of what he was seeing with his own, red-rimmed eyes, in one tiny and remote part of his brain, like a man determined to show bravery in front of the firing squad, the denture-less Colm knew he had to salvage some shred of self-respect:

"Whabever banshee you ahh – this is a twihck, a cheap phehrground illushhun! If I *weally* fought you'd come back and haun me every nighd, then I'd hab to beliebe that bigs can *fly* – hahahahaha!!!"

But the laugh died in Colm's throat faster than a speeding bullet. Colm's blanky was suddenly whipped away. There, hovering between floor and ceiling was Paddy, wearing Colm's favourite hat…and with his very own dentures crammed into his mouth.

"Tomorrow, Colm Quigley", croaked Paddy with some difficulty with the dentures in, "When Tom O'Meaney arrives to seal this wicked deal with you, you will tell him that you have changed your mind and have no *intention* of forcing Mrs McGuirk from her house and there's not a chance in a million that you will allow him to build a sausage factory on her land – not now, not *ever* – is that understood?"

By now, poor Colm's brain was barely working - and the power of speech had *completely* deserted him.

All he could do was nod.

"Is that a '*yes*'?"

Colm nodded again, his mouth open, lips moist and a drop of snot ripe and ready to fall from the tip of his bulbous, purple nose.

"Good. If you keep your word, I will never visit you again. *But* if you break it – then woe betide you; no matter how many bolts you fit to any door, I shall make every night a living hell!"

Colm didn't hear any more because he collapsed in a dead faint there and then.

* * *

At 8 o' clock the following morning, Colm's bedroom door creaked open, and Grace McMannus shuffled in, as she did every morning, with a cup of lukewarm tea and a single 'Arrowroot' biscuit.

"It's uppy-time, Colm", she croaked and opened the heavy red drapes just an inch or two, so as not to upset her employer any more than necessary. Grace was well-used to Colm snarling and growling at her during this age-old ritual, but not this morning. Instead, Colm was on the floor, crammed into the corner of his room with his knees up to his chest and his blanky wrapped tightly around him.

"Goodness me, Colm – you'll catch your death of cold down there! *Whatever's* the matter?"

"Hab you seen a big anywhehh ?", whispered Colm, his eyes darting anxiously around the room.

"A what? A *pig*?! Of course not! Now stop being a big baby and drink this lovely cup of tea that I've gone to all the trouble of making you."

The cup rattled against the saucer as Colm tried to drink it. No sign of a pig anywhere…and his dentures were still in the glass beside his bed.

As he noisily slurped down the tepid liquid, he began to feel calmer…. and the more he thought about it, foolish.

"Perhaps…perhaps", he mumbled to himself, "all is *not* lost…I've been under a bit of strain lately. Maybe I've just been getting the heeby-jeebies because of that? In a few hours' time, I'll hand O'Meaney a signed agreement…we'll shake on it, and then it's game over for that annoying old bag and her trick pony of a pig. It's that crook O'Meaney's problem after that – *I'll* be out of sight an hour later and no dancing sheets or flying pigs will ever be able to find me!"

And with that slightly happier thought uppermost in his mind, Colm set to work: after hastily washing and shaving – and managing to leave just a few stray tufts of bristle below his left ear – he climbed into the cleanest clothes he could find, wolfed down the cold & rubbery bacon sandwich Grace had left for him under a plate in the kitchen and headed into the front parlour, where he kept his desk.

And scattered amongst all the bills, invoices, and final demands, he found a copy of the *Notice to Quit* agreement that was the key to his future health, wealth & happiness. All it needed now was some signatures…and there, like a miracle, staring right at him, was the answer: a faded old bank cheque from Mrs McGuirk that he'd forgotten to cash…with her lovely, simple child-like signature in the bottom right-hand corner…

"This must be a sign!", he hooted - and he set straight to work trying to copy it.

20 minutes later, he was in his rusting old van, hurtling pell-mell towards his pub. He still had plenty of time to clear up last night's unwashed glasses and find someone he could persuade to 'witness' the precious document sitting snugly inside his jacket pocket.

Moments later, Colm was tentatively unlocking the front door of the saloon bar. Slipping inside…he eased the door quietly shut behind him.

But turning round to survey the damage – he was met with an extraordinary sight: instead of the piles of unwashed glasses and dirty tables he was expecting – the entire place was spick and span – cleaner, in fact, than it had been for years!

"How could this *be*?", he wondered aloud. "The whole place was a tip when I left here last night…".

And then, like the sun rising at dawn, Colm began to understand what must have happened: there was no talking, singing, or flying pig…no dancing blanky, nothing unusual *at all*, in fact. He must have cleaned all this by himself after *drinking* too much…it wouldn't be the first time! Which must mean, that the pig should be *still* down in the cellar!

Scarcely daring to believe that every terrible thing he had experienced in the last couple of days was no more than an horrific nightmare, Colm took a deep breath and slowly slid back the bolts on the trapdoor behind the bar. Opening it just an inch, he peered down into the gloom below.

Staring right back at him were the two innocent and frightened eyes of Paddy the pig.

Colm's heart *soared*!!!

He wasn't mad – the pig was – well, just a *pig*. And in his pocket, was the signed 'Agreement' that sealed Mrs McGuirk's fate – and secured *his* future!! Excitement & bravado surged through Colm like an electric current.

"Well? What have you got to say for yourself now, you dimwitted porker? You don't scare me one teensy weensy little bit. You're not singing any more – are you?!"

Paddy continued to peer blankly up at his tormentor for a moment longer, then let out a small grunt, turned and shuffled away towards a distant corner of his gloomy prison.

CHAPTER 14
St Joseph's Rest Home For The Weary

Colm slammed the trapdoor shut and let out a 'whoop!' of delight.

"I'm not going mad… and I'm going to be rich…and important…and famous! Everyone will want to know me once I'm rid of that old lady and her stupid, *stupid* pig!!!"

At that very moment, the saloon bar door crashed open and an expectant Tom O'Meaney strode into the bar.

"Well, Quigley – do we have a deal – or not?!", barked O'Meaney.

"Haha – we do indeed!!", chirruped Colm, feeling on top of the world as he did so…a man feeling that life simply couldn't get *any* better!
"What'll you have, Tom?", asked Colm as he reached up for the single malt his customers could never afford.
'We're Irishmen – a couple of Bushmills' will do the trick!"

While Tom was savouring his first slug of Ireland's finest, Colm, with a triumphal smirk, slid over the precious *Notice to Quit* …

"It still needs a 'Witness' signature, but that'll be no problem," soothed Colm. 'It'd better not be", O'Meaney shot back. Get someone in here and let's get this over and done!"

"Oh, don't worry about that, fellas – *I'd* be happy to do it. And why don't we have another drinkie while I do the honours?"

The two men snapped their heads round as if one person – their grins frozen.

All that could be heard was the ticking of the giant wall clock over the bar's fireplace...

And there, hovering in mid-air behind the bar wiping a glass with a tea towel was Paddy the Flying Pig.

"Same again, lads? Or maybe a couple of pints of Guinness…with some cheese & onion crisps?"

The shouts & screams of the two men were initially drowned out by an enormous crash: their shoelaces had been tightly tied together and they were now face down on the floor, struggling to disentangle themselves…

As the two men reached the pub door together – a tug of war with it began. To no avail. It was locked from the outside. As they frantically shook it for all they were worth, shouting for help all the while – Paddy was suddenly there – hovering right behind them:

"Ah, *c'mon* fellas – will you not have another drink? It's on the house, *promise*!"

But the only response Paddy could make out from either man was a sort of 'Yeaaaaaarghhhhahhhhhhhh!' sound.

Paddy had *never* had such *fun*.

For the next few minutes, he chased both men around the empty saloon bar, as they tried hiding under tables, or behind curtains…a couple of times letting them think they were safe before sneaking up behind them and whispering, "There you *are* Colm!' or "*Yoo hoo*, Tom – funny place to hide!" He even tried a joke or two: "Hey, Quigley – what's a foot long and slippery? A slipper!!! Geddit?"

But while all this racket was going on, neither Paddy, nor his two terrified victims heard the approaching police sirens. And in another few minutes, Colm & Tom's shouts for mercy were interrupted by a loud, official-sounding banging on the pub door.

"Open up!! It's the Garda here! What's going on in there?"

A minute later, a key could be heard turning in the giant lock outside – and the familiar, imposing figure of Officer Michael C. Cassidy filled the doorframe. But before he could say a word – he was knocked backwards by two hysterical, shouting & shoeless men rushing to get out:

"A pig…a pig…a pig…flying…talking…. *pig*…!!!!!", they shouted over each other, gasping and frothing and generally making no sense at all to the bemused officer, who thought he'd seen it all….'til now:

"Whoa there, fellas – caaaaaaalm down! You're making not a *jot* of sense… how much have you been drinking, for God's sake? Now – one at a time….".

But neither Tom O'Meaney or Colm Quigley could make Officer Michael C. Cassidy understand hardly a single word they were saying – especially as they were shouting and pointing.

"A pig, you say? Well, these lovely gentlemen out here are here to help you… why don't you say 'hello' to them, while I take a quick look around inside here, OK fellas?"

As Colm & Tom allowed themselves to be meekly led towards a white van with a red cross on it, Officer Cassidy strode into the pub with two of his subordinates.

"Take a look around, lads – we're on the lookout for a *very* dangerous pig, apparently", his sarcasm not lost on the smirking PC's Duff and Byrne.

A sizeable crowd had, by now gathered outside the pub, including a highly agitated Mrs McGuirk and an excited Aidan.

"Has anyone found my pig – Paddy?! I'm sure he was kidnapped by *that* dreadful man, Colm Quigley!!", she shouted to the assembled throng, pointing at the by-now semi-hysterical landlord.

A murmur of disapproval rippled through the 30-40 eager bystanders, all craning to see a protesting Quigley and O'Meaney being roughly squeezed into a pair of straightjackets & shoved into the back of the waiting hospital van.

A few 'boos' could be heard and several shouts of 'Good riddance Quigley!' and 'If you've hurt a hair on Paddy's head, Quigley – you'll know all about it!' - while some of Mrs McGuirk's friends tried to calm her down, each promising her yet another cup of tea and a slice of cake as soon as this ordeal was at an end – no matter *how* it turned out.

Inside the pub, each door had been opened, curtains pulled back and tables looked-under. Eventually, young PC Duff called out:

"Over here, sir! there's a *trapdoor….*".

While officer Cassidy towered over his two subordinates, they slid back the trapdoor's bolts and peered into the gloom below…and there sitting quietly, sitting on top of what looked like some sort of legal document, was a pig.

"This must be him, sir – he looks like a harmless devil. What shall we do with him?" "Get the poor fella up here and have that shouting woman out there take him home with her – since she seems so upset about it."

As Paddy was re-united with a sobbing Mrs McGuirk and a beaming Aidan, the assembled crowd led by a very excited Mac McCardle broke into applause. A reporter and photographer from the *Drogheda Bugle* scrambled to capture the story of the brave, kidnapped pig who was – almost certainly – '*…moments away from a sticky end at the hands of two scheming crooks.*'

And since it was almost opening time, and Officer Cassidy was in no hurry to return to the station to tackle the pile of paperwork in his in-tray, he – along with dozens of thirsty onlookers – piled into *Quigley's Bar* with the sole intention of draining it dry.

And just as Mrs McGuirk whispered to Paddy that it was high time they went home; they paused just long enough to see a white van pulling away, en route to *St Joseph's Rest Home for The Weary*, with two faces pressed up against the rear windows shouting something neither Mrs McGuirk, Paddy or Aidan - could *quite* make out.

* * *

That evening, Mrs McGuirk's house was a riot of music, dancing, drinking and laughing. The fairies made more noise than Mrs McGuirk imagined possible – *and* more mess!

Noggin was there, red-nosed and smiling his toothless grin…the secret friend and protector of the fairies. Aidan was allowed to stay up a *little* later than usual, and was being teased by nearly everyone about it being 'a long way back to Tipperary'. Paddy was asked to tell the same story over and over about how he chased Colm and Tom around the bar…the King made sure everyone was reminded that it was thanks to *him* granting Paddy magic powers that it had been possible to thwart two wicked men…and Mrs McGuirk even made a (slightly tearful) speech about being happy, truly happy amongst her new friends and…most importantly of all, having safely back home…her oldest and dearest friend: Paddy.

Paddy the Flying Pig.

The End

About the author

Caius has spent the last 4 decades producing, directing and scripting factual television for every UK broadcaster (and a few US ones) on everything from bag ladies to ventriloquists and from sabre tooth tigers to cheating in sport.

He is an occasional voice over artist
(https://codavoice.com/voices/caius-julyan/)
and has lived in London all his life – and still visits his beloved relatives
in his mother Eithne's village…of Termonfeckin.

This story is inspired by my father Ron's bedtime stories
to my sister Alex and I.

Paddy The Flying Pig: The Audiobook
as read by Allan Keating is available on Kindle

Follow me on Instagram: @caiusjulyan

Paddy The Flying Pig will return soon.

Printed in Great Britain
by Amazon

73836554-ab94-4fbb-990f-b22d50d60570R01